0 to 10

by Bobby Lynn Maslen
pictures by John R. Maslen

Scholastic Inc.

New York • Toronto • London • Auckland • Sydney • Mexico City • New Delhi • Hong Kong • Buenos Aires

No part of this publication may be reproduced, stored in a retrieval system, or transmitted in any form or by any means, electronic, mechanical, photocopying, recording, or otherwise, without written permission of the publisher. For information regarding permission, write to Scholastic Inc., Attention: Permissions Department, 557 Broadway, New York, NY 10012.

Copyright © 1999 by Bobby Lynn Maslen. All rights reserved. Published by Scholastic Inc. *Publishers since 1920.* Published by arrangement with Bob Books® Publications LLC. SCHOLASTIC and associated logos are trademarks and/or registered trademarks of Scholastic Inc. BOB BOOKS are trademarks and/or registered trademarks of Bob Books® Publications LLC.

Lexile® is a registered trademark of MetaMetrics Inc.

48 47 46 45 44 43   23 24 25 26

Printed in China 68
This edition first printing, October 2020

Zed had O (zero) beds.

Too bad, Zed.
O beds.

Pop had 1 top hat.

Pat had 2 fat cats.

Tom met 3 big cops.

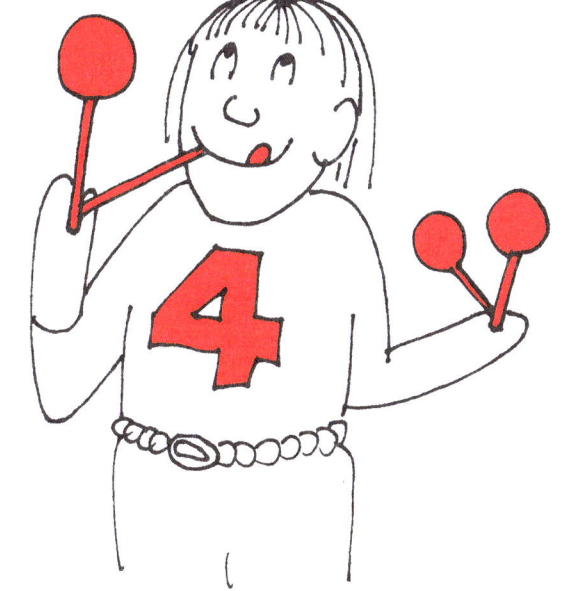

Lil had 4 lolly-pops.

Ron saw 5 wet rats.

Pam saw 6 big hats.

Peg had 7 pet hogs.

Bet met 8 bad dogs.

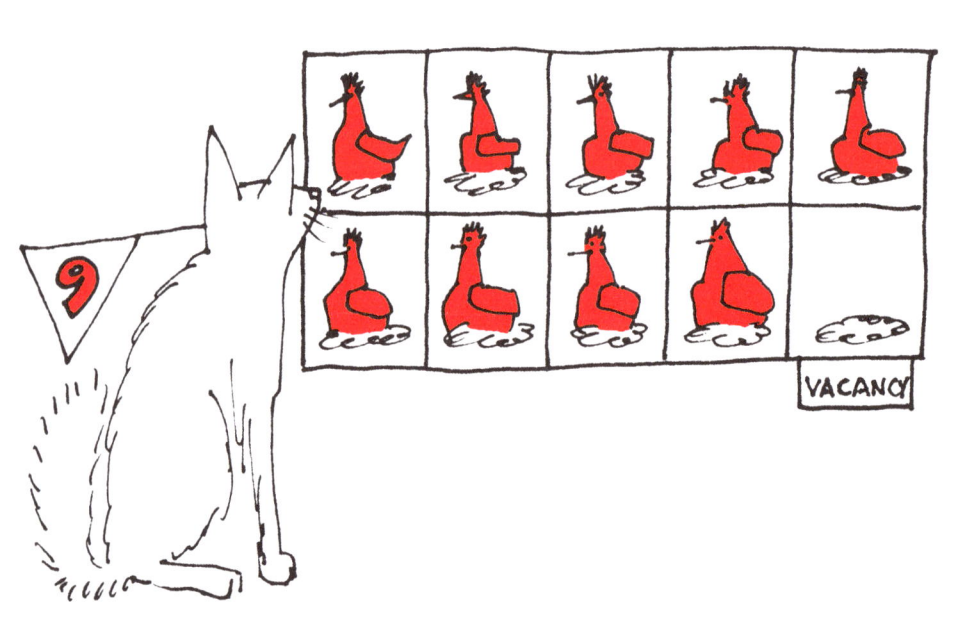

Sox saw 9 red hens.

Ben met 10 big men.

Ten was at......

10

The End

List of 41 words in 0 to 10

Short Vowels

Aa	Ee	Ii	Oo	sight
at	bed	big	cop	hi
bad	Ben	Lil	dog	saw
cat	Bet		hog	the
fat	end		lolly-pop	to
had	hen		Pop	too
hat	men		Ron	was
pal	met		Sox	zero
Pam	Peg		Tom	
Pat	pet		top	
rat	red			
	ten			
	wet			
	Zed			

Sam

by Bobby Lynn Maslen
pictures by John R. Maslen

Scholastic Inc.

New York • Toronto • London • Auckland • Sydney • Mexico City • New Delhi • Hong Kong • Buenos Aires

Beginning sounds for Book 2:

C c — cat

D d — dog

No part of this publication may be reproduced, stored in a retrieval system, or transmitted in any form or by any means, electronic, mechanical, photocopying, recording, or otherwise, without written permission of the publisher. For information regarding permission, write to Scholastic Inc., Attention: Permissions Department, 557 Broadway, New York, NY 10012.

Copyright © 1976 by Bobby Lynn Maslen. All rights reserved. Published by Scholastic Inc. *Publishers since 1920.* Published by arrangement with Bob Books® Publications LLC. SCHOLASTIC and associated logos are trademarks and/or registered trademarks of Scholastic Inc. BOB BOOKS are trademarks and/or registered trademarks of Bob Books® Publications LLC.

Lexile® is a registered trademark of MetaMetrics Inc.

48 47 46   22 23 24

Printed in China 68
This edition first printing, August 2020

Sam and Cat.

Mat and Cat.

Sam, Mat, and Cat.

Cat sat on Sam.

Mat sat on Sam.

Sad Sam. Sad Mat.

Sam sat. Mat sat.

O.K., Sam. O.K., Mat. O.K., Cat.

The End

Available Bob Books®:

My First Bob Books® Alphabet
My First Bob Books® Pre-Reading Skills
Set 1: Beginning Readers
First Stories
Rhyming Words
Advancing Beginners
Sight Words Kindergarten
Animal Stories
Sight Words First Grade
Word Families
Complex Words
Long Vowels

Dan's Plan

by Lynn Maslen Kertell
pictures by Dana Sullivan

Scholastic Inc.

No part of this publication may be reproduced, stored in a retrieval system, or transmitted in any form or by any means, electronic, mechanical, photocopying, recording, or otherwise, without written permission of the publisher. For information regarding permission, write to Scholastic Inc., Attention: Permissions Department, 557 Broadway, New York, NY 10012.

Copyright © 2013 by Lynn Maslen Kertell. All rights reserved. Published by Scholastic Inc. *Publishers since 1920*. Published by arrangement with Bob Books® Publications LLC. SCHOLASTIC and associated logos are trademarks and/or registered trademarks of Scholastic Inc. BOB BOOKS are trademarks and/or registered trademarks of Bob Books® Publications LLC.

Lexile® is a registered trademark of MetaMetrics Inc.

28 27 26 25 24 23 22   23 24 25 26

Printed in China 68
This edition first printing, July 2013

Dan ran and ran.

Dan was hot.

Dan got a cap.

Dan was hot.

Dan had a plan.

Dan got a fan.

Dan got a tub and a can.

Not hot now, Dan!

The End

Word Family: AN

can
Dan
fan
plan
ran

Other words in this story:

a	hot
and	not
cap	now
got	tub
had	was

Cam's Snack

by Lynn Maslen Kertell
pictures by Dana Sullivan

No part of this publication may be reproduced, stored in a retrieval system, or transmitted in any form or by any means, electronic, mechanical, photocopying, recording, or otherwise, without written permission of the publisher. For information regarding permission, write to Scholastic Inc., Attention: Permissions Department, 557 Broadway, New York, NY 10012.

Copyright © 2013 by Lynn Maslen Kertell. All rights reserved. Published by Scholastic Inc. *Publishers since 1920.* Published by arrangement with Bob Books® Publications LLC. SCHOLASTIC and associated logos are trademarks and/or registered trademarks of Scholastic Inc. BOB BOOKS are trademarks and/or registered trademarks of Bob Books® Publications LLC.

Lexile® is a registered trademark of MetaMetrics Inc.

28 27 26 25 24 23 22   23 24 25 26

Printed in China 68
This edition first printing, July 2013

Cam wants a snack.

Can Cam get jam?

Pam has jam.

Can Cam get a yam?

Gram has a yam.

Can Cam get a clam?

Pam has a clam.

A snack for Cam is eggs and ham.

The End

Word Family: AM

Cam
clam
Gram
ham
jam
Pam
yam

Other words in this story:

a	get
and	has
can	is
eggs	snack
for	wants

The Hen in the Den

by Lynn Maslen Kertell
pictures by Dana Sullivan

Scholastic Inc.

No part of this publication may be reproduced, stored in a retrieval system, or transmitted in any form or by any means, electronic, mechanical, photocopying, recording, or otherwise, without written permission of the publisher. For information regarding permission, write to Scholastic Inc., Attention: Permissions Department, 557 Broadway, New York, NY 10012.

Copyright © 2013 by Lynn Maslen Kertell. All rights reserved. Published by Scholastic Inc. *Publishers since 1920.* Published by arrangement with Bob Books® Publications LLC. SCHOLASTIC and associated logos are trademarks and/or registered trademarks of Scholastic Inc. BOB BOOKS are trademarks and/or registered trademarks of Bob Books® Publications LLC.

Lexile® is a registered trademark of MetaMetrics Inc.

28 27 26 25 24 23 22   23 24 25 26

Printed in China 68
This edition first printing, July 2013

The hen was in the den.

Ken was in the den.

"Go in the pen, hen."

The hen did not go in the pen.

Ten men went to the hen.

The hen went in the pen.

The hen sat on a nest.

The hen had eggs.

The End

Word Family: EN

den
hen
Ken
men
pen
ten

Other words in this story:

a	in	the
did	nest	to
eggs	not	was
go	on	went
had	sat	

The Red Sled

by Lynn Maslen Kertell
pictures by Dana Sullivan

Scholastic Inc.

No part of this publication may be reproduced, stored in a retrieval system, or transmitted in any form or by any means, electronic, mechanical, photocopying, recording, or otherwise, without written permission of the publisher. For information regarding permission, write to Scholastic Inc., Attention: Permissions Department, 557 Broadway, New York, NY 10012.

Copyright © 2013 by Lynn Maslen Kertell. All rights reserved. Published by Scholastic Inc. *Publishers since 1920.* Published by arrangement with Bob Books® Publications LLC. SCHOLASTIC and associated logos are trademarks and/or registered trademarks of Scholastic Inc. BOB BOOKS are trademarks and/or registered trademarks of Bob Books® Publications LLC.

Lexile® is a registered trademark of MetaMetrics Inc.

28 27 26 25 24 23 22   23 24 25 26

Printed in China 68
This edition first printing, July 2013

The red sled sped.

It sped on a hill.

It hit a shed!

Get up, Ted.

Get up, Fred.

Go to bed, Fred and Ted.

Put up your leg. Get a rest.

Fred and Ted get back on the sled.

The End

Word Family: ED

bed
Fred
red
shed
sled
sped
Ted

Other words in this story:

a	hit	the
and	it	to
back	leg	up
get	on	your
go	put	
hill	rest	

Bug and Pug

by Lynn Maslen Kertell
pictures by Dana Sullivan

Scholastic Inc.

No part of this publication may be reproduced, stored in a retrieval system, or transmitted in any form or by any means, electronic, mechanical, photocopying, recording, or otherwise, without written permission of the publisher. For information regarding permission, write to Scholastic Inc., Attention: Permissions Department, 557 Broadway, New York, NY 10012.

Copyright © 2013 by Lynn Maslen Kertell. All rights reserved. Published by Scholastic Inc. *Publishers since 1920*. Published by arrangement with Bob Books® Publications LLC. SCHOLASTIC and associated logos are trademarks and/or registered trademarks of Scholastic Inc. BOB BOOKS are trademarks and/or registered trademarks of Bob Books® Publications LLC.

Lexile® is a registered trademark of MetaMetrics Inc.

28 27 26 25 24 23 22   23 24 25 26

Printed in China 68
This edition first printing, July 2013

Bug has a jug.

Bug tugs on the jug.

Pug has a rug.

Pug rolls on the rug.

Pug has a mug.

Pug tugs on the jug.

Pug has the mug and the jug.

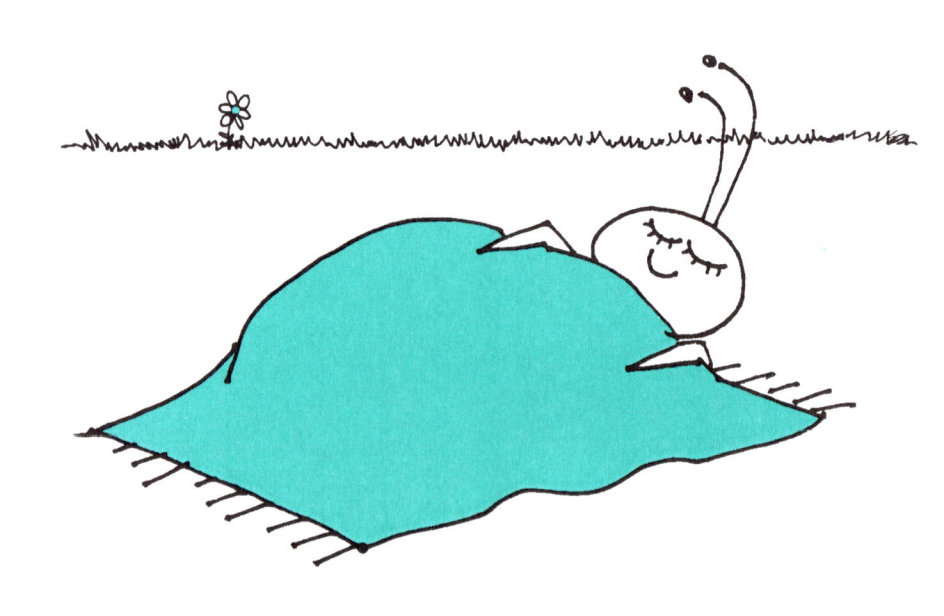

Bug is as snug as a bug in a rug.

The End

Word Family: UG

Bug
jug
mug
Pug
rug
snug
tugs

Other words in this story:

a	is
and	on
as	rolls
has	the

In a Huff

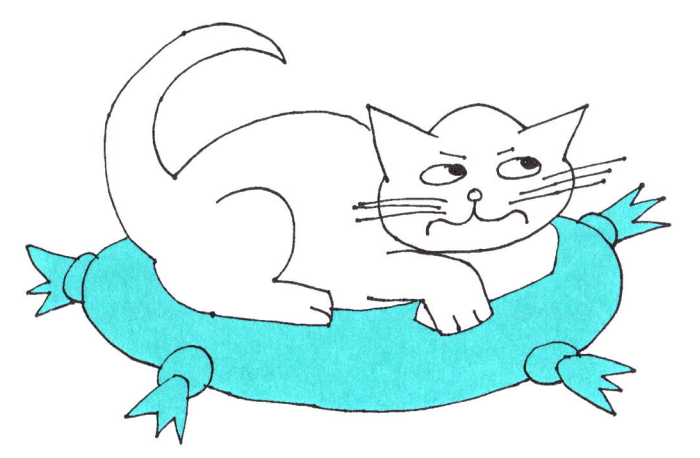

by Lynn Maslen Kertell
pictures by Dana Sullivan

Scholastic Inc.

No part of this publication may be reproduced, stored in a retrieval system, or transmitted in any form or by any means, electronic, mechanical, photocopying, recording, or otherwise, without written permission of the publisher. For information regarding permission, write to Scholastic Inc., Attention: Permissions Department, 557 Broadway, New York, NY 10012.

Copyright © 2013 by Lynn Maslen Kertell. All rights reserved. Published by Scholastic Inc. *Publishers since 1920*. Published by arrangement with Bob Books® Publications LLC. SCHOLASTIC and associated logos are trademarks and/or registered trademarks of Scholastic Inc. BOB BOOKS are trademarks and/or registered trademarks of Bob Books® Publications LLC.

Lexile® is a registered trademark of MetaMetrics Inc.

28 27 26 25 24 23 22   23 24 25 26

Printed in China 68
This edition first printing, July 2013

Muff is a cat.

Muff is in a huff.

Ruff runs. Ruff tags.

Ruff is too gruff.

Muff is stuck.

Muff has a plan!

Fluff! Puff!

Muff purrs.

The End

Word Family: UFF

fluff
gruff
huff
Muff
puff
Ruff

Other words in this story:

a	is	tags
cat	plan	too
has	purrs	stuck
in	runs	

The Spot

by Lynn Maslen Kertell
pictures by Dana Sullivan

Scholastic Inc.

No part of this publication may be reproduced, stored in a retrieval system, or transmitted in any form or by any means, electronic, mechanical, photocopying, recording, or otherwise, without written permission of the publisher. For information regarding permission, write to Scholastic Inc., Attention: Permissions Department, 557 Broadway, New York, NY 10012.

Copyright © 2013 by Lynn Maslen Kertell. All rights reserved. Published by Scholastic Inc. *Publishers since 1920.* Published by arrangement with Bob Books® Publications LLC. SCHOLASTIC and associated logos are trademarks and/or registered trademarks of Scholastic Inc. BOB BOOKS are trademarks and/or registered trademarks of Bob Books® Publications LLC.

Lexile® is a registered trademark of MetaMetrics Inc.

28 27 26 25 24 23 22   23 24 25 26

Printed in China 68
This edition first printing, July 2013

Dot has a doll.

The doll is on the cot.

The doll is in the pot.

The doll got a spot.

No, no, not a spot!

Dot rubs the spot.

Dot rubs the spot a lot.

No spot on the doll, Dot!

The End

Word Family: OT

cot
Dot
got
lot
not
pot
spot

Other words in this story:

a	no
doll	on
has	rubs
in	the
is	

The Dog in the Fog

by Lynn Maslen Kertell
pictures by Dana Sullivan

Scholastic Inc.

No part of this publication may be reproduced, stored in a retrieval system, or transmitted in any form or by any means, electronic, mechanical, photocopying, recording, or otherwise, without written permission of the publisher. For information regarding permission, write to Scholastic Inc., Attention: Permissions Department, 557 Broadway, New York, NY 10012.

Copyright © 2013 by Lynn Maslen Kertell. All rights reserved. Published by Scholastic Inc. *Publishers since 1920*. Published by arrangement with Bob Books® Publications LLC. SCHOLASTIC and associated logos are trademarks and/or registered trademarks of Scholastic Inc. BOB BOOKS are trademarks and/or registered trademarks of Bob Books® Publications LLC.

Lexile® is a registered trademark of MetaMetrics Inc.

28 27 26 25 24 23 22   23 24 25 26

Printed in China 68
This edition first printing, July 2013

A dog jogs to a bog.

The bog is full of fog.

The dog finds a frog.

The frog is in the fog.

The dog finds a hog.

A log is in the fog.

The dog gets on the log.

The dog, frog, and hog jog on the log.

The End

Word Family: OG

bog
dog
fog
frog
hog
jogs

Other words in this story:

a
finds
full
is
of
on
the
to

Lin in the Bin

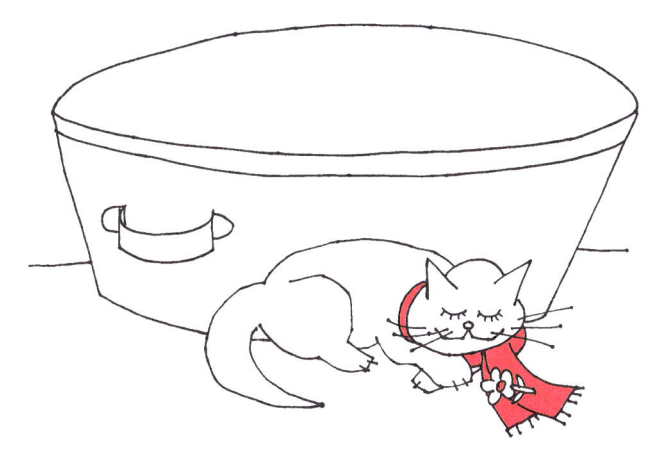

by Lynn Maslen Kertell
pictures by Dana Sullivan

Scholastic Inc.

No part of this publication may be reproduced, stored in a retrieval system, or transmitted in any form or by any means, electronic, mechanical, photocopying, recording, or otherwise, without written permission of the publisher. For information regarding permission, write to Scholastic Inc., Attention: Permissions Department, 557 Broadway, New York, NY 10012.

Copyright © 2013 by Lynn Maslen Kertell. All rights reserved. Published by Scholastic Inc. *Publishers since 1920*. Published by arrangement with Bob Books® Publications LLC. SCHOLASTIC and associated logos are trademarks and/or registered trademarks of Scholastic Inc. BOB BOOKS are trademarks and/or registered trademarks of Bob Books® Publications LLC.

Lexile® is a registered trademark of MetaMetrics Inc.

8 27 26 25 24 23 22   23 24 25 26

Printed in China 68
This edition first printing, July 2013

Lin is in the bin.

Lin has a pin.

Lin can spin and spin.

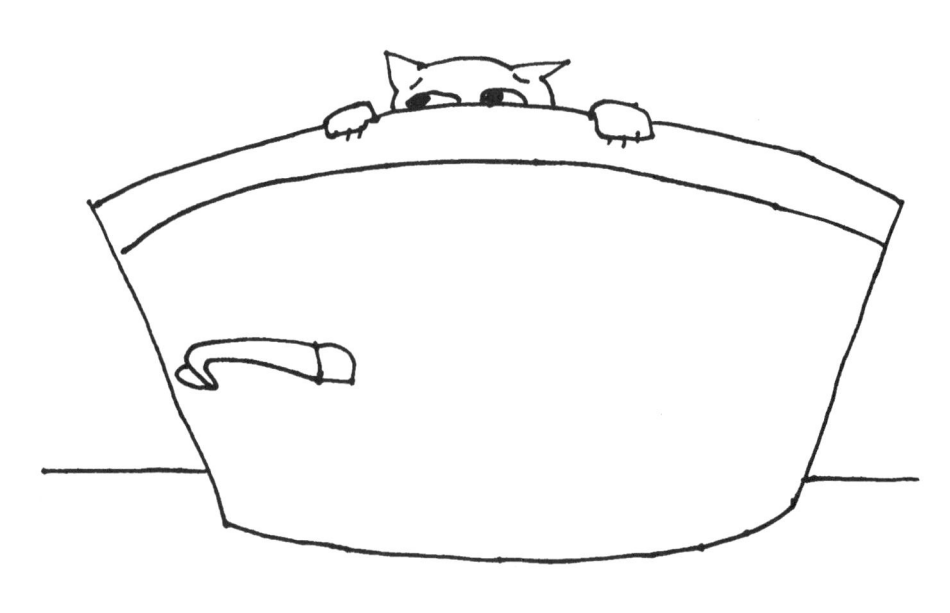

The bin is tin.

Lin is in a fix.

Lin did a flip and a skip.

The bin did tip.

Lin did grin.

The End

Word Family: IN

bin
grin
Lin
pin
spin
tin

Other words in this story:

a	fix	is
and	flip	skip
can	has	the
did	in	tip

Drip, Drip, Drip

by Lynn Maslen Kertell
pictures by Dana Sullivan

Scholastic Inc.

No part of this publication may be reproduced, stored in a retrieval system, or transmitted in any form or by any means, electronic, mechanical, photocopying, recording, or otherwise, without written permission of the publisher. For information regarding permission, write to Scholastic Inc., Attention: Permissions Department, 557 Broadway, New York, NY 10012.

Copyright © 2013 by Lynn Maslen Kertell. All rights reserved. Published by Scholastic Inc. *Publishers since 1920*. Published by arrangement with Bob Books® Publications LLC. SCHOLASTIC and associated logos are trademarks and/or registered trademarks of Scholastic Inc. BOB BOOKS are trademarks and/or registered trademarks of Bob Books® Publications LLC.

Lexile® is a registered trademark of MetaMetrics Inc.

28 27 26 25 24 23 22   23 24 25 26

Printed in China 68
This edition first printing, July 2013

The sun is hot.

Kip and Jip run and skip.

Kip and Jip want a drink.

"Drip, drip, drip."

"Yip, yip, yip!"

Kip licks his lips.

Jip grins. Jip drags a pan.

Kip and Jip get a sip.

The End

Word Family: IP

drip	sip
Jip	skip
Kip	yip
lip	

Other words in this story:

a	licks
and	pan
drag	run
drink	sun
get	the
grin	want
his	was
hot	